For Uton Hinds, the Irie One—G.H.

For Rowan, Doctor Bird's biggest fan—A.W.

DOCTOR BIRD

Three Lookin' Up Tales from Jamaica

GERALD HAUSMAN

ASHLEY WOLFF

PHILOMEL BOOKS · NEW YORK

How Doctor Bird
Taught Mongoose a Lesson
that Mongoose Never Remembered

One day Doctor Bird saw Mongoose steal an egg from under Mrs. Hen's nose. Then he saw her take a melon from Farmer Donkey's crocus sack, and a cho-cho from the garden of Brother Rooster. She was busy, Mongoose was, stealing things from everyone.

Perhaps I ought to teach our friend Mongoose a lesson, Doctor Bird thought. So he went into the bush and took a

nutmeg in his mouth and flew over Mongoose's house and dropped it on the roof.

The nutmeg struck the tin roof with a bang, which woke Mongoose from her nap. Mongoose rolled her eyes and snorted, "Rattling and banging noise, go away!"

Then she went back to sleep.

Now, as everyone knows, Doctor Bird is capable of making magic. So he ordered Nutmeg to bounce underneath Mongoose's bed and cause a terrible racket. At once Nutmeg rolled under the bed and banged loudly against the bed springs.

Irritated, Mongoose woke up. Her eyelids flickered. Her nose sniffed. "What's this I smell?" she asked. "Cornmeal pudding with nutmeg?"

Then she reached under the bed, snatched the nutmeg and swallowed it whole. After that she went back to sleep.

Doctor Bird saw what had happened. So he plucked a long cerasee vine off a banana leaf and commanded it to wrap around Mongoose and tie her up tighter than a tick's hatband. Instantly, Cerasee Vine did as Doctor Bird said.

"Hey, what's happening to me now?" Mongoose cried as she tried to hop out of bed. Cerasee Vine had her bound up, wrapped up, and rolled up, and she couldn't move at all. But, as everyone knows, Mongoose has sharp teeth, and it wasn't long before she used them. Snipping and snapping, she soon freed herself from Cerasee Vine's embrace.

Then she hopped back into bed and went to sleep.

"I'll just have to use stronger magic," Doctor Bird said and soared back to his hammock house. He opened up his juju bag full of tricks and took up one of his bad-luck weather goofballs. One bounce and Doctor Bird could change the weather from good to bad, and from bad to terrible. This he did, by dropping the bad-luck weather goofball on top of Mongoose's roof.

Pom, pom, pom went the goofball as it hit the rusty tin.

"What's that—another nutmeg?" Mongoose said, pulling the bedsheet over her head. But just then the weather changed from good to bad, and from bad to terrible. The sun hid behind a cloud and it started to rain, then hail. Great big silver stones fell out of the sky, and they clanged and banged and bonged and gonged on Mongoose's tin roof.

"Can't a poor lady get any sleep around here?" Mongoose said. But she just pulled the sheet higher over her head.

That is when Doctor Bird zoomed home and fetched the worst weather goofball he had in his bag, and he made it rain sideways into Mongoose's house.

Now Mongoose sat up and paid attention.

"All right," she said. "I'll close my shutters."

So she did. But the rain came in between the shutter slats, and no matter what Mongoose did, she couldn't keep the worst weather out. Soaking wet and very angry, she walked onto her porch.

What do you know, it was snowing! A wintry wind blowing!

But it was snowing and blowing around Mongoose's house—and nowhere else.

"Oh, oh," she cried. "Surely this is a magic spell, which means that someone has it in for me."

Then she saw Doctor Bird zipping by and she called to him in her nicest, friendliest, and most charming voice. "Oh, Doctor Bird," she said sweetly. "Won't you come in and have a cup of my best hibiscus tea?"

Now everyone knows how much Doctor Bird enjoys hibiscus tea. So he called off the snow and the sideways rain, and the sun came out from behind the cloud; and everything was as it should be.

Mongoose poured the tea. "Why are you playing these tricks on me, Doctor Bird?" she said. "I thought we were friends."

Doctor Bird said, "We were, and are. But I think it's time you stopped stealing food from everyone."

Doctor Bird took a sip. "Ahh," he said. "Mongoose, you do make the best hibiscus tea."

Mongoose was offended.

"What food did I ever steal from anyone?"

So Doctor Bird
told her about
Mrs. Hen's egg,
Farmer Donkey's
melon and Brother
Rooster's cho-cho.

Mongoose knew
that she was
caught and there
was nothing she could do.

Anyway, Doctor Bird's magic was not
something to be taken lightly.
And the snow had not yet melted
off her porch.

"All right," Mongoose said.

"Call off your magic. I promise to behave."

"Do you promise
not to steal again?"

"I promise."

Bird drank his hibiscus tea, offered
[com]pliments, and flew off on his see-
[through] wings. And that was the end of
[Mongoo]se's borrowing days. For a little while,
anyway. You see, after a time,

Mongoose started back the way she
always was, is, and forever will be.
She borrowed a yellow yam from
Mrs. Boa and a mango from
Mr. Monkey. And she even
slipped off with a bar of pink
carbolic soap from Auntie Mosquito.

However, she always returns what she
borrows the moment it starts to snow.

**And if this story isn't true,
let the keeper of heaven's door
say so now.**

How Doctor Bird
Taught Mouse to Look Up
When He Was Feeling Down

Doctor Bird lived at the top of a Flame Heart Tree. He lived in a house made of leaves and grass and the softest, silkiest moss, on the island of Jamaica. Doctor Bird loved his house, which swung like a little hammock in the wind, but one day a powerful breeze came from the sea and plucked the leaves off the Flame Heart Tree. The sky changed from blue to green,

and from green to gray, and from [...]
was coming in.

Now the wind kept a growing and a h[...]
and covered the beach, and white ruffled waves climbed over
the rocks of the seawall and swept across the road. Well,
Doctor Bird had no place to go, so he held on to his hammock
house, which was swinging like a flag in the wind. All night
the wind whipped, the sea roared, the rain rained. And all
night Doctor Bird held on for dear life, waiting for the storm
to be over.

In the morning the sun shone gold upon the land. The wind died down and the sea went back where it belonged, and Doctor Bird heard Mouse crying, "I have no house; pity me, poor Mouse with no house!" Now Mouse was not so fortunate as Doctor Bird, whose house swung from a branch in a tall-tall tree. No, Mouse had a tiny house, a little hole in the ground. And now it was all full of seawater. "How will I live?" cried Mouse. "How will I feed myself?"

"The same thing I asked myself," said Doctor Bird. The two of them looked around and saw that the land was bare, brown and leafless, for the hard wind had torn down everything green that lived.

"Whatever will we do?" Mouse asked, wiggling his worry-worry nose.

"I know," said Doctor Bird, who was a very "upfull" fellow. "We must count our blessings and look up and not down!"

"That is easy for you to say," said Mouse. "But we Mouse people always have our noses to the ground, for that is where our food is."

Doctor Bird darted about; he went this way and that. His wings whirred and blurred and they went so fast you could see the sun shining through them. "You must look up, Mouse," he said cheerfully. "Not down."

Mouse shook his head.

"What's to look up about?" he asked. "My belly is empty and when I look up, all I see is empty sky, which reminds me that I am hungry."

"Then you are not looking up." Doctor Bird smiled. "What I want you to do is *really* look up!"

Now Mouse looked up to the leaves of a palm that had taken quite a beating from the wind. There were still a few fronds left, and in among them, a great fat, round, brown coconut.

"Ahh," Doctor Bird said. "Now you are really looking up."

"How can a tiny little mouse, namely me, get up there and chew through such a thick brown nut?"

Doctor Bird struck the air like a black lightning bolt, whizzing backward and forward, and coming very close to Mouse's ear. "If you can get through the hard," he hummed, "you can sip through the soft."

"Is this a riddle?" Mouse asked.

"Take it for what it is and it will fill your belly all the way to full," Doctor Bird replied.

Mouse scanned the tall coconut tree. There was the great brown nut, full of white meat and coconut water.

"What I would do for one little drink," he thought. "Oh, well, here goes nothing," he said.

"There goes something," Doctor Bird said.

Then Mouse tucked back his ears and went running up the coconut tree. Soon he was on top of the world— well, almost, anyway.

"Now what?" Mouse asked. Doctor Bird, suspended in the sky, looked at Mouse. "Now, nibble-nibble, all the way to the water inside that nut," he said, and Mouse began to chew through the outer shell of the coconut.

"That's it," Doctor Bird encouraged. "Keep going."

So Mouse nibbled through the top of the coconut and pretty soon he was looking into the well of white water inside. There was enough sweet coconut water to drink for several days, and enough jelly to eat for a week. But then he wrinkled his nose and wiggled his whiskers.

"What's wrong now?" Doctor Bird asked.

"How am I going to get a drink without falling in and drowning?"

"Remember what I told you before? Just look up. And don't look down." Doctor Bird zoomed into the sky. Mouse followed him with his eyes until he was looking straight up. As he strained to see Doctor Bird disappear into the blue air, his long, skinny mouse-tail dropped into the hole he'd nibbled.

"Something feels cold," he said in alarm. Quickly, he jerked his tail back up where it belonged.

"That's the idea," Doctor Bird said.

"What's the idea?" Mouse said. But already he'd figured out what Doctor Bird meant because mice, as we know, like to keep themselves very clean, and Mouse was no exception. As soon as he saw his tail was sticky and wet, he started to clean it off with his tongue.

"Ah, ha!" he cried. "That tastes good." And he dipped his tail back down into the hole.

After a while Mouse drank all the coconut water he could drink and he ate all the coconut jelly his belly could hold. And now what he wanted to do was have a good long nap, but of course he remembered that he didn't have a house anymore.

"Don't worry," Doctor Bird told him.

"You can sleep over at my house."

So Mouse spent the rest of that day and all of that night in Doctor Bird's hammock house up in the Flame Heart Tree. It was nice up there, Mouse thought, but he was a little afraid of falling when the wind blew. So Doctor Bird told him to tie his tail to the limb of the tree. That way he'd be sure to sleep, safe and sound.

"Thanks, Doctor Bird," Mouse said, "for all the things you did for me today."

Doctor Bird said softly, "You just did what I always do—you looked up instead of down."

Mouse looked up, once, at the yellow moon, winking through the dark leaves of the Flame Heart Tree, and he nodded. Then, folding his hands over his full belly, he went to sleep.

And if this story isn't true,
let the keeper of heaven's door
say so now.

How Doctor Bird
Taught Brother Owl that
It's Better to Be Who You Are
than Who You're Not

One evening Doctor Bird was going to a Guango Party, where all the animal people get together under the great Guango tree and sing the old songs and play the ancient ring games under the light of the moon. Now Brother Owl heard about the party and he wanted to go, but he wasn't invited.

The reason for this was that a long time ago, Brother Owl proved that he couldn't be trusted. He was told by the other animal people to watch over the Great Box of Mysterious Things. For some time he did this, but one day his curiosity got the better of him. He pried open the box to see what was inside.

Out of that box came Darkness and Duppies, which is to say, night and ghosts.

And the world has never been the same since.

But Brother Owl was not happy with the way the animal people always avoided him, so one day he told Doctor Bird how he felt.

"I wish I were something other than what I am," he said.

Doctor Bird, who is a riddler as well as trickster, said:

A horse is a horse

And a mule is a mule;

An owl is an owl

And a fool is a fool.

That means, of course, that you can't change what you are or who you are because you can only be that which you are, and that is what you were born to be.

the riddle meant, but Doctor Bird recited another riddle:

A lie is a lie
And a love is a love;
A pigeon is a pigeon
And a dove is a dove.

Now, everyone thinks that Brother Owl is smart because of his round wise eyes and his large curious face. But, actually, he is a dull-witted fellow, who sees much and understands little.

"Are you trying to tell me something?" he asked.

Doctor Bird chuckled and said, "Who the cap fits wears it."

By which he meant, as everyone knows, that advice which is well given should be well taken. But Brother Owl, you understand, was not bright. He just looked that way. He foolishly thought that Doctor Bird was telling him to go to the Guango party. So Brother Owl got himself a hat and a long coat with tails, just like Doctor Bird's. He got a fancy striped vest and a stiff, starched collar, and a gold tie. That night he went to the Guango party. Brother Rooster was playing dominoes with Sister Mongoose, and Mr. Monkey was playing Pass the Stone with Mrs. Hen, Brother Green Lizard and Uncle Galliwasp.

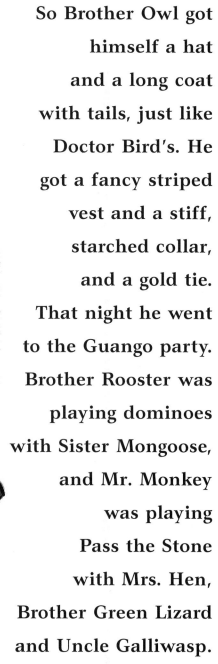

When Doctor Bird showed up, things really got going. He was dancing on air with merry old Mr. Pocket Parrot and singing songs with pretty little Miss Banana Quit, and everybody was having a grand time except Brother Owl, who felt left out, sitting all by himself on a lonely branch.

Maybe I ought to make myself known around
here, Brother Owl thought. So he did a jig and
a reel and he went round and round by himself.
By and by, his collar sprung into the air and flew
off. Next, his coattails got caught on a John Crow
vine, his fancy striped vest popped its
buttons, and his gold tie got hooked
on a pimento tree. Now, for the first
time, everyone could see who was
hiding under those party clothes. And
after they untied him from that branch,
they tried to pluck his feathers out.

Brother Owl flew off, yelling that he was going to hoo-doo all the people at the Guango party. But he was lucky to get out of there with his feathers still stuck to his tail.

And ever since that night, Brother Owl has been a loner who lingers in the night woods, and he comes out only when everyone else has gone to bed. He'd be mighty lonely too, if it weren't for the night animals, who come around to console him from time to time. There's Brother Blinky, the firefly, Sister Croaker, the gecko lizard, and Auntie Ratty Batty, the fruit bat.

Every once in a while, when the trumpet flowers are blooming in the early hours of the morning, Doctor Bird shows up and offers Brother Owl a riddle like this one:

A flea is a flea
And a fowl is a fowl;
A fly is a fly
And an owl is an owl.

By which everyone understands—but especially Brother Owl—that it's better to be who you are than who you're not.

And if this story isn't true,
let the keeper of heaven's door
say so now.

AUTHOR'S NOTE

The Doctor Bird, the national bird of Jamaica, is found nowhere else in the world. Some believe the male (which has the special plumage and tail) to be the most beautiful hummingbird there is. Imagine him in a shaft of golden sunlight, his foot-long tail forking like black lightning; or perhaps like an eighteenth-century doctor's frock coat, flying in the wind.

In addition to the beauty of the Doctor Bird, he is believed to possess some kind of magic, the power to heal and make whole, and the power to cast a spell. The old folk song goes, "Doctor Bird's a cunny bird, hard fe dead." This means "Doctor Bird's a clever fellow, who's hard to kill." The Arawak Indians, the original natives of Jamaica, called him "the bird of God." For it was believed that when a man died, his spirit went into the Doctor Bird and lived there forever.

These stories are from the north coast of Jamaica and the small town of Port Maria in the parish of St. Mary. The principal storytellers are Roy McKay, Benji Oswald Brown, Mackie McDonnough, Charles Davis, and Pansy Douglas. This is their book, as much as the Doctor Bird is their sprightly, mystical companion.

GERALD HAUSMAN

Patricia Lee Gauch, editor.
Text copyright © 1998 by Gerald Hausman. Illustrations copyright © 1998 by Ashley Wolff.
All rights reserved. This book, or parts thereof, may not be reproduced in any form
without permission in writing from the publisher, Philomel Books, a division of
The Putnam & Grosset Group, 200 Madison Avenue, New York, NY 10016. Philomel Books,
Reg. U.S. Pat. & Tm. Off. Published simultaneously in Canada.
Printed in Hong Kong by South China Printing Co. (1988) Ltd.
Book design by Cecilia Yung and Marikka Tamura. The text is set in Garth Graphic Bold.
The art for this book was done with black gesso and gouache on Arches cover.

Library of Congress Cataloging-in-Publication Data
Hausman, Gerald. Doctor Bird : three lookin' up tales from Jamaica /
Gerald Hausman ; illustrated by Ashley Wolff. p. cm.
Summary: Three stories featuring Doctor Bird, the clever, positive-thinking hummingbird
found only in Jamaica. 1. Tales—Jamaica. [1. Folklore—Jamaica.] i. Wolff, Ashley, Ill. II. Title.
PZ8.1.H29Do 1998 398.2'097292'04528764—dc21 [E] 97-9610 CIP AC
ISBN 0-399-22744-X
1 3 5 7 9 10 8 6 4 2

First Impression